Glenisheen

By David Ryan

First Published on 22 August 2010

By Lulu Publishing

3101 Hillsborough Street, Raleigh, North Carolina, NC 27607

www.lulu.com

© 2010 The Author.

The right of the author to be identified as the author of this material has been asserted in accordance with The Copyright, Designs and Patents Act 1998.

All rights reserved. No part of this book may be reprinted or reproduced or utilised in any form of by any electronic, mechanical or other means, now known or hereafter invented, including photocopying and recording or in any information storage or retrieval system, without permission in writing from the author.

Typeset in Arial by author

Ireland as a county is world renowned for its storytelling. This has been a part of the culture for many generations. There are many tales; some tell of the natives, some tell of the invaders and some of the folk that hide behind the veil behind the rain or in the shadows away from humankind. All of these people have brought their own story to the misty landscape of Ireland and their influence has shaped the landscape itself. Some of the tales are very well known, for example the legend of how a certain giant named Finn McCool built the Giant's Causeway to reach his adversary in Scotland. However, there are many stories that only exist in a whisper or their telling depends on the characters you will meet along the way as you make your travels through Ireland.

It was Easter time in the year 2003 that a group of student friends and I happened to find ourselves in the village of Spidal, just outside Galway. This may seem like a strange name for a place. However, we had learned that the name came from the fact that at one time an infirmary was to be found in the area, and rather than take the time to talk about the 'infirmary', as the Irish tended to be economical with the use of descriptive words, the name was changed initially to 'hospital' and then further shortened to just 'Spidal'. The building that housed the infirmary had long gone and to look at the bundle of buildings that gathered together to call themselves Spidal, one would find it difficult to imagine that a hospital ever was located there.

It was a strange day, we had been requested by our Professor to go into the surrounding countryside and map what farmers were growing in the fields. The Professor Hanglands or simply 'Prof' as we liked to call him was a strange character at the best of times, not being renowned for his stature he usually stomped his way in a purposeful manner on field studies, stopping seemingly at random to offer his pearls of wisdom on whatever geographical feature he had stumbled upon. He had this knack of appearing to be surprised by his findings, only we knew that he had been leading these field studies for years and that these locations had become known as 'Hanglands Hotspots' Some of the hotspots deserve mention for their amusement value. One time the Prof requested the assistance of some of the students who had been known to play rugby to help him up on a picnic table where he proceeded to hold court in a dramatic way by delivering his thoughts on a drumlin that had no business being where it was. On another occasion he highlighted the significance of a monument that had been placed in a tourist area, but was sculpted to resemble a part of the human body – the rest can be left to the imagination of the reader.

Prof rarely changed his appearance, having a bald head on top and yet long locks of grey hair down each side of his face. He was of the old school who enjoyed wearing a plain white shirt, corduroy tie and corduroy jacket complete with sewn on brown elbow patches. His trousers were grey and no matter what the season of the year his feet were shod with Moses sandals and grey woollen socks. Just occasionally as a concession to relaxation the top button of his shirt would be opened, but this was only at the end of the day when the 'business' was complete.

The Prof wore tortoise shell glasses at all times and on top of these balanced two busy white eyebrows. We knew little of the Prof except for his cult status in the University and the characteristics he displayed which always amused the students. He had the knack of making the driest subjects interesting with amusing anecdotes, and the students often questioned whether or not the anecdotes had any basis in truth or not. *'There is no need to let the truth get in the way of a good story'* he would often quote, but never acknowledging the source of the quotation.

There was some talk of the Prof being a leading light in Rhodesia at some stage but due to the politics of regime change he was kicked out and therefore found himself in Ireland. Some considered that he had been awarded an MBE or OBE along the way for his troubles but the truth or otherwise of this remained a mystery.

The area where we were studying was an Irish speaking one or Gaeltacht and there had been an interesting event over the course of the day when some farm children approached us and asked us what we were doing, only in turn to be chastened by their father for speaking English. No doubt he thought that as we were carrying clipboards and recording data that we may have been from a Ministry of some sort in Dublin and were seeking out the farms where the children spoke English rather than Irish and whether or not the Irish language was being used where it should have been. The confusion that a clipboard can cause!

After we had spent our day counting potatoes and cabbages and potatoes and carrots and potatoes and potatoes we more or less knew what was being grown in the fields around Spidal – Potatoes. An interesting fact that we discovered that day was that in some parts the soil in the fields was too shallow to grow potatoes. This being Ireland the situation was obviously regarded as being unacceptable to the people, they put their heads together to creatively get around the problem by lifting half the soil from a bed and dumping it on top of another bed to create something called a 'lazy bed' – with just the right amount of soil to grow potatoes. By the end of the day the potatoes around Spidal were declared to be fit and healthy and we retired to the village.

Some of our party headed for a local hostelry for refreshment whilst others including myself sat outside watching the rays of the setting sun perform dances on ripples of the water of Galway Bay. As we rested we were joined by some of the locals who had also retired to the village after a day tending the very potatoes we were so interested in. In was not long before we were admitted to their conversations.

'Fine Day?'

'That it is' I replied.

'A fine day for doing what you were doing then?' the stranger continued.

'Yes indeed it was' I responded, enjoying this game whereby he really wanted to know what our interest was in potatoes but without actually having to use the words 'tell me what you were doing then'. So as not to allow this to end in a standoff and perhaps cause come offence I decided to be direct.

'I am sure that you wonder what we were up to today then.' I asked.

'Aye, well some would wonder about that'. Replied the stranger and paused.

I decided to let the pause hang in the air for a little while and while this was happening I took the opportunity to consider the stranger. He was what one might describe as a typical Irish man, standing just over five foot tall, with a mass of grey wavy hair that gave no hint as to of the colour it had ever been. His face was a little rounded and clean shaven. His chin was interesting in that it appeared to have been added to his face at a later stage to the rest of his body being formed as it appeared bulbous giving him a mischievous air. He was wearing a pair of black boots, grey trousers with a brown belt and a grey tweed jacket over a red woollen jumper with a checked shirt and orangey brown tie. In some respects he resembled the picture postcard image of an Irish man; all he was missing was a pipe and a Shillelagh!

The stranger picked up the reigns of the conversation, and as if he had read my thoughts took a pipe out of his pocket which he held in his hand as he continued the conversation.

'On the other hand some may not really care at all' he said, and continued 'but in these times, with a Northern accent like yours it may just be useful to give a hint of what you were about'. The stranger placed an emphasis on the 'just' and he was clearly referring to the Troubles in Northern Ireland. I thought it useful to end the mystery.

'Believe it or not, we are all university students from Belfast and we are here on a field study looking at crops' I said, perhaps giving more information than what I intended to do at first.

'Now that is interesting' said the stranger, with just a subtle hint of sarcasm.

Obviously exhausted from his efforts at conversation, a lull developed. One of my friends decided to address the silence.

'Hello, I'm Gabriel' he said, offering the stranger his hand.

'Well Gabriel, it is good to meet you' said the stranger, without providing a name.

'David' I said, holding out my hand which he took and shook.

'Pleasure' he said, obviously not caring to provide us with his name. He then took a pipe from his pocket, filled it with tobacco, pushed it down and then skilfully lit the pipe with a match, managing to shield the flame from the gentle breeze. A blue hue of smoke started working its way heavenwards. The stranger seemed to be contemplative and after a while he continued.

'This is the land of poets and scholars, I am sure that you know that' he said. 'I assume you being students that some of you will be scholars. What I really want to know is if there are any poets or writers among you?'

We all looked at each other in bewilderment. This was not a twist in a conversation that would have been expected at that juncture.

'Why do I ask this I can hear your think?' said the stranger, 'well, let me tell you' he added as he took the pipe from his mouth and pointed it in the direction of the water in the bay.

'I have just been thinking. Are there any of you who can write? What words would you use to describe what you see in front of you?' he asked as he jabbed his pipe in the direction of the water in the bay.

More of our group had joined us now and we all looked over Galway Bay. After a period of reflection we began suggesting words that may describe the landscape. 'Magnificent' said Maurice, 'stately' said Liam; 'Magic' said Gabriel (with a broad Belfast accent).

'No! No!, No!' said the stranger, 'all these words don't even begin to capture what lies before your eyes. Think again!'

New words started to emerge 'sparkling sea' said Eamon, 'shimmering…ness' I added.

'The whole point is that what you see in front of you cannot really be described. It is all of the words that you have used, but each of these words only addresses a small part of the whole. The Bay is its own person, with a personality, with many faces and she is clothed in different garments at different times of the day' said the stranger.

'That's poetic' said Gabriel.

'That's because I am a poet' replied the stranger, but the whole point of the matter is that painters try to paint Galway Bay, and photographers take pictures, musicians compose songs and sing ballads, and poets think of words. No one of use can capture the whole picture or the whole story, we can only describe the bit that we see without own limited skills, and just when you think that you've caught her, doesn't the light change and then she's different again and you have to start all over again' said the stranger.

'Whao!, that's deep' said Gabriel, as he turned his back on the Bay and began walking back to the row of shops 'way too deep for me!' he said under his breath but not so as to allow us to hear.

'I am old and have been trying to catch the words to describe her all my life and have not even come close' said the stranger turning to face me. I noticed that his eyes were wet with tears.

'Every time I see a new group in the village, I hope that someone will have brought me the words I need, but this hasn't happened yet' he said.

'I think that she has great mysteries and that she will only tell them to those that she trusts' I said, feeling that I had managed to use words to describe something of the beauty that lay before us in the now setting sun.

'I really think that you are beginning to get it David' said the stranger. I was surprised that he had remembered my name.

'Let us retire to McDermott's window, there is a turf fire and a good view of the Bay' said the stranger, as he turned and walked across the road. Of the 10 or so of us that had gathered to hear him wax lyrical about Galway Bay, myself and three others followed him.

'Next thing they will give Galway Bay a flipping woman's name, just like the Annie Liffey' said Eamon. He always was cynical and I hoped that the stranger hadn't heard him as that sort of negativity could spoil what was turning out to be an amazing moment.

'What will it be then Ben? asked the bar tender as we went in, giving away the secret of the strangers name.

'The usual' he replied as he was handed a pint of Guinness that surely must have been pre-poured for him.

Within a few minutes we were all settled in McDermotts, some of our party with Guinness in hand whilst others clasped their hands around hot mugs of coffee.

 Then Ben said. 'I am going to begin to tell you a tale, and I want you to bear with me. This tale has never been told before and it must be told now. Part of the reason you cannot describe the Bay is that she holds deep and dark secrets. My tale will let you into some of the secrets that I mention. I must tell you of the Glenisheen.' And so he began to address us in an authoritative voice,

This story does not and cannot start in a 'once upon a time' fashion as you may be misled into thinking that the story of the Glenisheen is some sort of fairy story and I can assure you that this is most definitely not the case. The other problem with 'once upon a time' is that would assume there was a beginning to the Glenisheen and that is not a claim I can make as there is no point that could be ascribed as their beginning, and the story also covers many thousands of years and therefore cannot ever be 'once upon a time'

The Glenisheen were a race, but not a race of people and they were not creatures. Their existence must have lain somewhere between the two. To try to understand the Glenisheen you need to know something of their lifestyle and in particular how their lifestyle, landscape and being were so closely intertwined.

The Glenisheen lived many thousands of years ago in an area of Ireland that modern man calls The Burren. This can be found just to the south side of Galway bay if you want to go and look for it. This is a remote area and it was this geographical remoteness that enabled the Glenisheen to live their life in secret and to be well hidden. To be honest they were so well hidden that it was only recently their story has come to light.

The Glenisheen were a very small race of people, but yet not one of the 'little people' normally associated with Ireland. They reached only about a foot tall in height, but they were certainly by no means dwarves or Leprechauns, and they would become most annoyed if they were ever referred to as a dwarf or leprechaun as they were by in large not in possession of a beard. They had absolutely no resemblance to an Irish mythological creature that modern man would be familiar with and certainly would not be found on picture postcards for the tourists or have anything to do with crocks of gold. The wealth of the Glenisheen was found in other ways.

For clothing the Glenisheen wore a cape with a hole at the top for their head to protrude from. This was worn over an undergarment which was usually black in summer and white in winter. Occasionally some Glenisheen would wear whatever colour took their fancy in a particular morning; regardless of the season of the year they happened to find themselves in. Glenisheen of this nature were regarded with some suspicion and on occasions were best left alone. All Glenisheen went barefoot which resulted in them having very strong feet.

Perhaps the most striking feature of the Glenisheen was the features of their face. They were all bald and had a countenance of something between a new born human baby and a dying man in agony.

No one really knows where this race of being came from or for that matter whatever befell them after the events that I will now relate.

The Glenisheen were bound very closely together as a race, mainly because there was no other social group quite like them with which they would be happy associating with. There was only the one race of Glenisheen to be found anywhere on earth and they lived in a settlement that was named after the people – Glenisheen. What is not known was whether the people were named after the settlement or the settlement was named after the people or if it was some deep tie that bound the two together in ways which could not be explained.

The settlement of Glenisheen was built as a defended city with strong walls all around. At the centre of the city where two objects of which the Glenisheen were justifiably proud, one was a well and the other was the bell in its tower. Although the walls of Glenisheen were made of sturdy stone this was not the case of the dwellings and public buildings in the city. Given the plentiful supply of wood from the forest and a lack of stone or rock in the vicinity, the predominant building material was therefore timber. Originally the buildings stated off as single storey but it was not so long before the pressure on space within the city walls necessitated the upward expansion of the buildings, and at the time of which is related, the buildings had reached in places three or four storeys tall. The Glenisheen were wise enough not to allow the height of the buildings not to exceed the height of the outer wall as they knew that this would leave them vulnerable. The only stone building in Glenisheen was the bell tower which did exceed the height of the walls as it was made of stone and therefore was considered to be of sufficient strength in times of attack.

Most of the dwellings in Glenisheen were located in the inside of the strong city walls with only but a few located outside the walls. The outside dwellings had mostly fallen into states of disrepair and been abandoned, ever since the 'troubles' with Kilcolgan had started. More will be said about this later. Beyond the city walls of Glenisheen were dense forests which were largely impassable to anyone, with the exception of Kilcolgan. The parts of the forest facing Glenisheen were not as dense as the rest of the forest and it was quite possible for the Glenisheen to walk for pleasure in these areas.

The plain between the city and the forest was rolling grassland and parts of this had been cultivated for farms to provide food for the Glenisheen. One of the interesting features of the Plain was that there was no water supply in the form of rivers or lakes to water the crops, and therefore the crops were dependent on the rain and the only water source for survival was the well in the centre of Glenisheen. Given the amount of rain in the west of Ireland irrigation for the crops was never required.

For a modern man looking at the dwellings of Glenisheen he could easily fancy himself as a Gulliver type character looking at a Lilliputian village or a collection of buildings with the appearance of dolls houses. In fact it has been rumoured in Ireland that Swift's ideas for Gulliver actually came from a mythical painting of Glenisheen which he found in the attic of an old house in Dublin.

For a modern traveller to desire to go the Burren to see what remnants of the Glenisheen may be found, they would be wasting their time as today the Burren looks nothing like it did during the inhabitation of the Glenisheen. Travellers will find that the Burren is a bland landscape which is formed mainly of limestone rocks. Very little of anything grows in the fields. Why fields one may well ask, as the area is largely unable to support crop growing and there is insufficient grass to raise cattle. For some unknown reason which goes back to prehistory the Irish have always been territorial and closely marked out the territory they claim to own. Visiting the Burren many people continue to question why it is the case that despite its barren nature that the field boundaries have been marked out with stone walls. The entire area closely resembles the surface of the moon and yet there are these field boundaries marked.

Part of the reason for the barrenness is the complete lack of water. Limestone is a rock which is known as porous, and that is exactly what happens to any water that has the misfortune to find itself there, it simply disappears as it pours straight through the rock and finds its way underground. For the traveller that cares to take the time to explore deep underground you can find caves carved out by the water and some amazing stalagmites and stalactites and rivers.

Unfortunately for any would be farmer the water is simply too far below the surface to have any use whatsoever for farming. Even if the water could be brought to the surface it is spoiled as it already has been contaminated by minerals as it found its way underground, and if the farmer was able to find an area with a small amount of soil, damage would quickly be done as the contaminated water would soon poison any crops or animals if not simply wash the whole lot away underground. The question could be asked as to where this forsaken place came from as it is located in the middle of fertile farming areas and there is no relationship of any kind between the two.

Apart from the Glenisheen themselves, there were only two other individuals who knew of their existence – one totally friendly, but yet not so friendly that he didn't do all that was within his power to defeat the other – the enemy of the Glenisheen- known to them by the terrible name of Kilcolgan.

The story of the troubles with Kilcolgan is a long and protracted one, apparently boiling down to either Kilcolgan invading the garden of the Glenisheen or the Glenisheen invading the garden of Kilcolgan. However, it was that long ago that nobody actually remembers and in consequence the exact trust remains unknown as both Kilcolgan and the Glenisheen have different versions of the same story.

So who or what was Kilcolgan? Kilcogan, was a giant who stood about 11 feet tall from the soles of his boots to the thatch of his mop of wild curly ginger hair that to some would resemble a birds nest as Kilcogan never combed his hair. It should be pointed out that the height of Kilcogan could only ever be an estimate, as certainly no Glenisheen would have had the courage to stop him whilst out for a walk on the plain and ask him to lie down in order to have his measurements taken, for quite simply that Glenisheen would have found himself being picked up and bitten in two for a snack for Kilcolgan. As for the humans, although Kilcolgan was only a few feet taller than the tallest human in the area, they would not dare approach him as to those who knew of him he was considered a wild animal of a giant.

There was never a Glenisheen that didn't shudder at the mention of Kilcolgan's name. Just consider, the Glenisheen were one foot tall and they stood barefoot, whereas Kilcolgan was eleven times their size in big boots. This was mainly due to the fact that they were around one foot tall and he was somewhere around eleven feet. To the Glenisheen looking upon Kilcolgan it would seem that he did reach the sky given that the poor Glenisheen had to strain his neck heavenwards to see the top of where Kilcolgan ended.

Kilcolgan chose to live in remote areas far away from mankind. The reason for this was simple, as giants were generally regarded by mankind as being creatures worthy of attack. The exact reasons for mankind's desire to harm a giant are not known, but may have had something to do with appetite. In those days a butchered pig could comfortably feed a human family for the best part of a year, and this was appreciated by the humans given the time and effort required to raise a pig from a piglet until such times as it was regarded as being large enough for eating. Translating the raising of a pig to giant language was a different matter. There were no such things as giant pigs and therefore when a giant felt hungry he really was left with no alternative but to eat two or three pigs for one meal. Traditionally the role of the giant was not to waste time raising animals for food, and why would time be wasted doing this when there was an ample supply of humans to perform that task. The giant's role became one where their task was to use their height as a weapon and simply approach human settlement and remove whatever livestock they saw fit whilst the humans were left shuddering in their farms afraid to challenge this bullying approach.

That might well have been the case originally when the humans were not good at fashioning weapons and the sticks and stones that would have been thrown at Kilcolgan had the ability to do little harm apart from knocking out the odd tooth.

Through time the humans discovered how to fashion weapons using different metals and these had the ability to do considerably more harm than the sticks and stones. Kilcolgan's temper and rage grew worse as the standards of the weapons improved and he went home from many a raid nursing puncture wounds to various parts of his body. These puncture wounds formed ugly scars which marred the appearance of Kilcolgan and made him look an altogether ugly being.

The humans soon developed the art of living in towns and villages rather than isolated farmhouses and with their weapons at the ready, Kilcolgan reached a stage in his development where he had to balance the need of food with the risks of maybe not coming back after a raid. His conclusion was to leave the humans well alone unless absolutely necessary, and instead identify a simpler source of food that would not bite back. That is why the Glenisheen became his target.

It was thought that at one time Kilcolgan had managed to form a relationship with a female giantess called Clara and for a time she tried to tame him into having a less aggressive outlook on life. However, the story goes that due to a shortage of food that Clara had died and not only had her attempts to quell Kilcolgan's anger failed when they were together, but her death only contributed to making him worse than he was in the first place.

Kilcolgan lived in a cave overlooking the Atlantic Ocean, where most nights he would sit and watch the sun sinking in the west over Galway Bay and think of his days with Clara and when food was plentiful. Kilcolgan knew that in his cave he was safe as no human could approach the case from the sea or from the land above. This was a relief as on occasions Kilcolgan had been chased away from Human settlement by gangs armed with metal weapons intent on killing him.

Some would imagine that living so close to the sea would have its advantages in terms of feeding the hungry giant. This was not the case as far as

Kilcolgan was concerned. On occasions Kilcolgan would notice the humans going out to sea using small rowing boats and casting nets into the sea and bringing up fish. Kilcolgan had not managed to use what limited mental capacity he had to translate his observations into practical activities. He seriously considered that fishing was beyond his capabilities as he continually put up a number of obstacles to fishing. Some days he would convince himself that he didn't know how to build a boat and even if he did, as the human boats usually put to sea with more than two rowers, he didn't know where to find other giants that would help him row. On other days he would look at the human's fishing nets. He had a fear of these as on one raid to the human settlement to steal livestock he had got caught up on some nets that were drying on the shore, and this had caused him to crash to the ground, landing on his face and losing his two front teeth for his trouble. Kilcolgan certainly didn't want anything to do with nets.

The other excuse that Kilcolgan made continually to himself was that he could not wade into the water as he didn't know just how deep it was and he carried visions in his head of his mouth and nose disappearing underneath the water and him never coming back up again. Needless to say Kilcolgan could not swim and he had a real fear of water.

Kilcolgan had tried eating some fish once or twice that he had found in boxes beside the shore. This had caused him many problems – to fill his stomach he had to eat a lot of fish. The fish that he ate (box and all) he found very salty and he was tortured with a thirst. The only water he had to hand was that in the ocean and that is what he drank. Needless to say this did not ease his thirst and instead drove him quite mad. Given these negative experiences fish were most certainly off Kilcolgan's menu.

When Kilcolgan was with Clara she had encouraged him to take pride in his dwelling and ensure that food remains were removed from the cave rather than being left to fester in dark unlit corners. Clara had also encouraged some husbandry by getting Kilcolgan to start a farm at the top of the cliff where vegetables were planted and some cows and pigs raised. However, all this soon feel into states of disrepair following Clara's death as Kilcolgan in a fit of rage ate all the life stock over the period of a few weeks without thought as to what his food source would be when the farm animals were no more.

Some think that the troubles between the Glenisheen and Kilcolgan were due to one or the other raiding one or the other's farmland at some stage. The exact trust is unknown but the timing of the start of the troubles was reckoned to be sometime following the supposed death of Clara.

There was another possible reason for the long enmity between Kilcogan and the Glenisheen and that was in relation to the Glenisheen Bell. At one stage Clara had made a warm hat for Kilcolgan for use during the winter months, not so much as to keep his head warm as his wild mop of ginger curly hair was quite capable of doing this, but to keep his hair on one place and stop it blowing into his eyes when it became wet. The hat was successful in this enterprise.

Kilcolgan had another major problem with his hair during the summer months, given his fear of water and lack of a comb, his hair would never have been washed. This resulted in his hair attracting birds, either seeking to nest directly in his head or seeking to remove parts of the hair for use as nesting materials. To try to overcome these problems Clara had fitted a bell to the top of Kilcolgan's hat, the idea being that the sound of the ringing bell would deter the adventures of any birds that flew in the direction of Kilcolgan's head. At least that is what Clara told Kilcolgan as she encouraged him to continue to wear what was a winter hat with a tinkling bell during summer months. Secretly Clara had another plan that any human would was in the vicinity of Kilcolgan's food raids would hear him coming and take the necessary precautions to get out of the way and preferably take his livestock with him. The hat was also successful in this enterprise as Kilcolgan invariably had to return to the enterprise of farming for his sustenance rather than rely on taking other peoples.

When Clara died Kilcolgan was totally distraught, especially considering that her death was essentially his fault as he had not been able to provide for them both through farming. In a fit of rage Kilcolgan tore off his hat with the bell and threw it as far as he could into the forest late one spring day. The hat caught in a tree as it made its fall and it hung there in the breeze. Kilcolgan had no desire whatsoever to go through the thick forest to retrieve the hat and in fact never wanted to see it again.

It was during that same summer that some young Glenisheen teenager lads had had ventured into the forest with their girl folk seeking a place of isolation to discuss future relationships. By that stage the birds and elements had removed most of the fabric from what had been Kilcolgan's hat and all that remained was the bell, still held in the trees by a few remaining threads. The bell went unnoticed until a gentle breeze stared to blow and the bell announced its prescence to the party below. One of the party was the son of the ruling Tullagh, and fearing what the noise and object may mean he ran back to his father, forsaking Susan the girl folk he was with and summoned his father and several other elders of Glenisheen to come to the forest.

On arrival at the forest beneath the bell, the Glenisheen soon mounted a rescue whereby some of the more nimble Glenisheen climbed the trees and rescued the bell from its perch by means of cutting the remaining fibres of what had been Kilcolgan's hat and lowering the bell to the ground. The Glenisheen carried the bell back to the city in a triumphant procession whilst the teenagers and girl folk proceeded behind in a somewhat sullen fashion as their discussions on future relationships had been interrupted.

The Glenisheen regarded the bell as a gift and built a sturdy stone tower in the centre of the city beside the well in which to house the bell.

The Glenisheen had fought many battles with Kilcolgan and Kilcogan had fought many battles with the Glenisheen. Every time a battle was fought it was the strength and size of Kilcolgan that meant he had never been defeated. Again, the version of the story differs from the perspective of whoever is telling it. In the account of Kilcolgan it was the Glenisheen that attacked him whereas in the account of the Glenisheen it was Kilgolgan who initiated the attack.

The other person I have mentioned in this account of the Glenisheen was fortunately friendlier than Kilcolgan. This 'other person' was a mystical figure that inhabited the land at that time that was held in some awe by the Glenisheen. In the mind and conversation of the Glenisheen he was simply referred to as 'The Master'. His real name was a mystery to all concerned. In the battles between Kilcolgan and the Glenisheen, The Master remained a neutral figure, although it was well known that he secretly supported the Glenisheen (unofficially off course).

For many of the Glenisheen The Master was a character that existed only in the minds of some. And in consequence he was thought of as a charter that could be used to frighten the children into behaving – something akin to a bogey-man in the realms of human existence. The fact of which the Glenisheen remained unaware was that The Master was more or less responsible for the very existence and survival of the Glenisheen people.

I have already mentioned that the people were very close and the extent of this can be seen from their list of Chieftains. Every last one of them was called Tullagh, right back to The Great Tullagh or Tullagh the First who was remembered for the writing of the law and prophecy for the Glenisheen. It was recorded in the Annals of Glenisheen that the law was written before the Glenisheen emerged as a race, and it was the law that shaped their being. Some people considered that The Great Tullagh was actually The Master.

One of the Laws of the Annals of Tullagh as written by Tullagh the First was that one the night of the death of the serving Tullagh an election was to be called during the time of mourning to elect the new Tullagh. In this was the Glenisheen would not be without a leader for very long. He election would consists of a number of candidates, including the eldest son of the dead Tullagh, eleven other candidates and a token candidate drawn from the ranks of the simpletons of Glenisheen. The amazing thing was that in every election it was always the eldest son of the previous Tullagh that would be elected the next Tullagh. It was considered by the Glenisheen that this was a good thing as no provision had been made in the law for what would happen if the eldest son would not be elected.

The Great Tullagh had granted a special gift to the Glenisheen that the first born child would always be a male. This meant that succession and inheritance was always a simple matter – passing onto the eldest son.

Originally all Tullaghs kept their succession numbers, but after many thousands of years the count became lost. It was thought that this was sometime around the leadership of Tullagh the 6789th or was it Tullagh the 6790th? The only time the law was changed was around that time when the ruling Tullagh became known as Tullagh the Old and his son Tullagh the Young. To avoid confusion it was written into the law that Tullagh the Young was not to have any children until such times as he became Tullagh. However, it turned out that this law was not able to be enacted as Tullagh the Young's could not help but providing Tullagh the Olds with a long series of grandchildren. The Master then intervened and ensured that only two Tullagh's would ever be alive at the same time. The other thing which transpired was that the family from whom the Tullagh's were elected, which was once known by some other long forgotten family name ultimately just used the surname Tullagh.

Gifts from 'The Master' to the Glenisheen have already been mentioned, and these were only some of the many gifts The Master bestowed upon the Glenisheen, all of which affected their lifestyle. One of the first of the gifts given had traditionally caused confusion, mainly because some say that if it was The Master who gave the gift to Tullagh the First then clearly Tullagh the First could not have been The Master as it is not possible to give and receive a gift to yourself as that would defeat the whole purpose of it being a gift. For those who believed that Tullagh the First was The Master no other explanation was usually forthcoming as to where the gift came from. The first gift of which I speak was that the firstborn child of every Glenisheen would be male and in that way the family names would never disappear. Other gifts included that there would be good harvests whilst Tullagh ruled the Glenisheen – which as you may already have ascertained would be forever, although it is not really known what the harvests consisted of or what their diet was. Old age was another gift and perhaps the most important gift of all was that the Glenisheen could understand any other language, whereas no one else would understand the language of the Glenisheen. This may be another reason as to why their existence remained so secretive for generations.

The Glenisheen did not keep calendar days in the way that we would be used to, but would have counted the days of the reign of each Tullagh. Bearing in mind what has been said already about the large numbers of Tullagh's there were, it really became a most confusing system when Glenisheen would talk about the four thousand, five hundred and fiftieth day of the reign of Tullagh the six hundred and forty seventh. Or 4550 of 637. In the end a simpler system was adopted whereby the Glenisheen would talk about just the number of dates of Tullagh the Old. They were happy to live with only one set of large numbers whilst they considered a better way to count their days, and to come up with a new system it was considered better not to rush decisions of this nature to make sure that any change would be for the better.

The particular Tullagh of which we are concerned with in this account (which must be taken as true) had just been elected Tullagh following the death of his father. He was full of mixed emotions – sadness over the death of his father, worry over how the election might go as nothing is guaranteed in life and fear and trepidation at the prospect of having to rule the Glenisheen until his own death, whilst at the same time nurture and cherish his son (Tullagh the Young) in preparation for the day when he would in turn come to rule the Glenisheen.

Tullagh decided the best thing to do in preparation for his rule was t go for a long walk in the woods during which time he could gather his thoughts and form a strategy for ruling the Glenisheen and finally defeating Kilcolgan. As he walked he was sad and during one of the moments of sadness he looked down at his feet and spotted a wishbone which was from an animal in the human world called a chicken, although Tullagh knew not from whence it came, although he heard of wishbones – as a national shortage had been highlighted in that when humans found them they kept breaking them for no apparent reason. Tullagh throughout nothing more of this and simply picked up his wishbone and placed it in a pouch inside his cloak.

About an hour later along the path Tullagh came across a dwarf sitting on a log by a clearing. The dwarf looked bedraggled and judging by the gasping sound he made suggested that he was in dire need of a drink, although no water was nearby.

Despite the fact that Glenisheen had no dealings with other creatures, Tullagh did stop and look at the Dwarf as he felt sorry for him.

'Please Great Tullagh, may I have a drink of water?' said the dwarf.

Tullagh could understand every word of the dwarf's language, but he did not find it strange in any way that a perfect stranger who he had never met would address him by name.

Tullagh thought about this request and considered that the only source of water he knew of was by now several miles away in the city of Glenisheen, and he could not recall passing any streams, wells, lakes or rivers on his journey. The reason for this was that the whole area on which the Glenisheen lived was on limestone which simply let water our through it to underground.

Then Tullagh turned his attention to the wishbone in his pouch. He had considered that if the wishbone was a magical one with wishing powers he could wish for a lot of things, like the defeat of Kilcolgan or wealth. As Tullagh was essentially a good hearted Glenisheen (a fact he had relied on during his election) he decided that the best thing to do in the circumstances was to try out the wishing powers of the wishbone for a flagon of water. He really did hope that this would work as he didn't relish the alternative of running back to Glenisheen for water or carrying the dwarf to the source of water.

Amazingly, the wish bone turned out to be one of the wishing variety and a flagon of water appeared beside Tullagh's side completely of its own accord.

He handed the flagon over to the dwarf who promptly drank all of it before disappearing himself in a similar way to that which had brought the flagon to Tullagh in the first place. 'That was quite ungracious' thought Tullagh to himself. 'he couldn't even say thank you or let me have a drop of water for myself' he considered. Tullagh out these thoughts out of his head and decided to resume his walk back in the direction of Glenisheen and turned his thoughts again to those that he had been having before the dwarf appeared.

Tullagh thought to himself 'Ah Ha!" as he continued his walk and as he did this he had not gone very far when he saw a shining figure standing before him.. At once Tullagh fell to his knees as he just knew in his innermost being that this mysterious figure could be no one else but 'The Master'. Tullagh shook in terror as the figure began to speak.

'Tullagh the New, arise and hear me" boomed the voice.

'He knows my name!' thought Tullagh as he slowly raised his eyes again in the direction of the figure and began a slow climb to his erect position.

'You are generous and kind of spirit Tullagh' continued the figure, although Tullagh didn't know where the conversation was going or what the figure was talking about. As if the figure had perceived Tullagh's innermost thoughts he said;

'I can come to you in many different ways, large or small, young or old, male or female, human or animal. Today I came to you as a thirsty dwarf.

Slowly Tullagh began to connect the two in his mind.

'y..y..y..you were the dwarf?' Tullagh asked in an unbelieving voice, not knowing how it could be the case that this enormous shining figure with a booking voice could be transformed from the dwarf with a small squeaky voice he had heard previously.

'I left the wishbone for you and wanted to test your mettle as the new leader of the Glenisheen, and when faced with the option of wishing for greatness or helping a fellow creature, you chose to be helpful' continued the figure.

'I know you don't know what I am referring to, but let me explain. As your heart has told you, my people the Glenisheen know me as The Master. I am he without beginning or end, who has been charged to ensure that no major harm befalls the Glenisheen' continued the figure. 'I have many names to many people but to you I am The Master'

Tullagh was terrified as his face turned whiter than what it had started when he first met the figure.

'Due to your generosity and kindness I am willing to make available a further gift to The Glenisheen'

Finding new boldness Tullagh interrupted The Master 'Destroy Kilcolgan' he said.

'You should know that your request is impossible for me to grant – that is not a gift, yet it is the one that every new Tullagh has asked me for when I meet him to commission his rule. I am all powerful but defeating Kilcolgan is not what I have in mind as a gift – which has to be given and received in a spirit of kindness and used for good' said The Master.

In reality The Master would have had the power to remove Kilcolgan from the face of the earth and enable The Glenisheen to live without the fear of his attacks. In some sense The Master felt that it was beneficial to allow Kilcolgan to continue his reign of terror to ensure that The Glenisheen remained focussed through their sense of fear, and that their belief in him as Master would not diminish. The Master debated these points with himself on a regular basis.

'The if only we could hide...or disappear...like..become invisible when Kilcogan comes to attack' stammered Tullagh, not realising that he was adopting a defensive stance when faced with the threat of Kilcolgan rather than as had been the case with his forebears to go and attack Kilcolgan and take the battle to him rather than waiting for the battle to come to him.

The Master had read Tullagh's heart and mind and drew from his robes a small blue bottle with a brown cork.

'Tullagh, when The Glenisheen come under attack you should eat bread and drink a small amount from this bottle.' Said The Master.

Tullagh accepted the bottle and opened the cork to smell the contents. It smelt like a deep red wine.

The Master continued. 'As soon as Kilcolgan is sighted you should do as I have commanded, and then sound the warning bell in the centre of the city'. You will find that the City and the Glenisheen will become completely invisible to all until such times as the danger has passed. One of the strange quirks of fate in this tale was that what had once been Kilcolgan's bell was now being used by the Glenisheen as a warning of Kilcolgan's attack. It may not be entirely surprising that during the attacks that whenever Kilcolgan heard the bell that it evoked memories of Clara and their time together. Therefore the sound of the bell enraged Kilcolgan the more, made him angrier than he was to begin with and intensified the strength and ferociousness of his attacks on the Glenisheen. At no stage did Kilcolgan come to realise that his missing bell was sitting in pride of place in the centre of Glenisheen, nor did he have any desire to try and retrieve the bell. On occasions he did wonder about what had happened to it but as far as he was concerned the bell had been lost for all time in the middle of the forest where it was too dense and thick to ever be found.

'Thank you oh great Master' said Tullagh, and was about to start waxing lyrical about how great The Master was and heaping on lots of praise when he found himself completely alone on the path. Tullagh reflected on the new gift and thought that this would go well with a previous gift from 'The Master', that when the Glenisheen were under attack from Kilcolgan, every last one of them would go so silent that no one would hear a sound and may just believe that they weren't there.

The day after Tullagh had met with The master, Kilcolgan learned from a dwarf (that he was about to eat) that the Glenisheen had a new Tullagh as the old Tullagh was dead. Kilcolgan reasoned with himself (insomuch as this was possible) that this was an opportune time to launch a new attack on the Glenisheen as surely they would be ill prepared, given that they may be either too sad to fight given the fact they were mourning the death of the old Tullagh, or be too drunk to fight in that they were celebrating the arrival of the new Tullagh. Kilcolgan also knew that it was important to launch an attack on the Glenisheen before they had time to meet with The Master and perhaps get a new gift from him which might just result in poor old Kilcolgan being defeated once and for all as the Glenisheen would become much too powerful for his liking.

It had been the custom and practice of the Glenisheen to mount a number of lookouts on tall trees around the edges of the dark wood, who could, if the time was appropriate raise the alarm of the coming of Kilcolgan. At first this had not been a successful enterprise as the only method of communication between the lookouts and the City required the lookout to climb down the tree and run across the plain as fast as his little legs would carry him, shouting at the top of his little voice that 'Kilcolgan was coming'. The usual result was that the first lookout to Spot Kilcolgan also became Kilcolgan's first snack of the day. This had necessitated devising some new way of the Glenisheen raising the alarm of Kilcolgan's arrival, whereby the City could be alerted and the lookout preserve his own life. The solution was found through the lookout keeping a pigeon beside him, which was released when Kilcolgan approached, and flew back home to the Tullagh's guardroom. When the pigeon arrived the defence of the city could be organised.

There was one famous legend in the annals of the Glenisheen that one foolhardy lookout forgot to bring provisions for his watch, and he got very hungry. He decided to write a note on a small parchment and attach this to the pigeon's leg to ask the guards to get his mother to bring some provisions, as he knew that he couldn't leave his post. The arrival of the pigeon callused alarm as the city prepared to defend itself against Kilcolgan's attack, only at the last moment to spot the note. Needless to say the foolhardy guard did get a visit from his mother, not with a basket of provisions but a stick to beat him around the head for his stupidity.

On the day in question a lookout spotted Kilcolgan striding through the forest towards the city of Glenisheen. Given the experience of the guard he immediately set about releasing his pigeon, but unfortunately the guard had just eaten his lunch and though that he would be kind and give his pigeon some crumbs from his bread.
Consequently, the poor pigeon was quite content to rest where he was, given his full tummy and really didn't see the point of flying back to Glenisheen to get some corn when he arrived. It was for this reason that the lookout had to shoo him off the perch and instead of flying back to the guardhouse, the pigeon started to flit and flap around the plain with no real sense of purpose.

The lookout realised the error of his ways and realised that it was highly unlikely that the pigeon would ever make if back to the guards in time for the city to prepare for the attack of Glenisheen. He was left with no option but to dismount from his tress and run across the plain, back towards Glenisheen. It was fortunate that he did remember from his training the absolute importance of not shouting at the top of his little voice as he was not desirous to become lunch for Kilcolgan. He was not able to run that fast as he had only recently finished his own lunch, but he did his best.

Thinks where not going well for the little Glenisheen lookout and it was fortunate that by this stage at least three other lookouts had also spotted Kilcolgan. Unlike our little friend they had not made the mistake of thinking they were being kind by feeding their pigeon as they knew that the real issue at stake was the need to be kinder to the Glenisheen by not feeding their pigeon. These lookouts were able to release their pigeons which flew with a strong sense of purpose back in the direction of the city of Glenisheen.

Even before the pigeons had landed in the guard house some sharp eyed guards had noticed the pigeons winging their way across the plan to converge on the guard house, and immediately set about running to the centre of the city to ring the warning bell.

It is a strange thing that one of the weaknesses of Kilcolgan was, in essence that he was not too sharp eyed. It was for this reason that he was never able to spot the pigeons crossing the plain, or if he did he would have soon snatched them from the sky and enjoyed them for another snack. What Kilcolghan lacked in eyesight he made up for in hearing, and one of the sure signs that he was on the right course to the city of Glenisheen was the ringing of the warning bell.

'Silly little things' he thought to himself, and so as the thought would not be lonely in his head he decided to have another one, 'so kind of them to ring their bell to let me know where to go'. As that was the limit of the thoughts that Kilcolgan could have at that time he had no more but simply continued towards the sound of the bell.

As for Tullagh, he had been roused into action by the sound of the bell and whilst his first thought was to run for his life, he remained calm under pressure and thought about what he had been instructed to do by The Master. 'Bread and Cake' he thought, 'no!, bread and wine, no, bread and bottle. Or was it bottle and tottle'. It really was incredible given the seriousness of the situation and the importance of the gift from The Master that Tullagh had not taken time to remember what he ought or even write the instructions down, and all the time Kilcolgan continued his march towards the Glenisheen. The strength of his footsteps were even starting to shake the foundations of the houses. The situation appeared hopeless.

It was just at this time when Tullagh really was of a mind to run when he heard in his head the words of the Master 'Bread and Bottle'. Tullagh them immediately started eating bread, carefully removed the bottle from the folds of his cloak and opened the lid. He took a small drink which had the effect of making him feel all warm on the inside and slightly dizzy. It was fortunate that he was able to put the cork back in the bottle and store it safely in his cloak before he noticed everything so transparent and see through. The entire city of Glenisheen had simply vanished from before his eyes, and he had too! In its place was a large grassy area that just resembled a continuation of the plain.

As for Kilcolgan, please don't think that he suddenly stopped in his massive tracks and had another thought along the lines of 'where has that city gone'. He simply continued to stride forward expecting to come across the city at any moment as he wasn't able to see it from the point he had reached, let alone realise that it had disappeared, and besides, his brain had more or less exhausted its store of thoughts for that day.

The Glenisheen were now invisible and silent. However, they realised that whilst the invisible state was beneficial, it also had its drawbacks as quite simply Kilcolgan could walk right over the top of the city and cause much destruction. Tullagh considered this point as he stared out across the plain. 'Typical gifts of the Master' he reasoned, 'whilst at one level they appear wonderful, they are never so perfect that they solve all ills' he continued with his thoughts 'nnnn not that I'm ungrateful' he said out loud, just in case The Master could have heard his thoughts and considered that he was indeed ungrateful.

What about Kilcolgan. He had attacked the Glenisheen so many times over so many years that he more or less knew then number of steps that he had to take from the edge of the forest, across the plain until such times as he reached the outer walls of the city of Glenisheen. Surprisingly he had never counted the number of steps involved nor the time it took to make the crossing. This was for two main reasons, he could not really count that well as he was too large to have ever gone to school (no school building was large enough to house him and he would have frightened the children, and quite possibly ate a few of them when he felt hungry) and he was usually too absorbed in thoughts of eating tasty Glenisheen by biting their heads off first.

Notwithstanding all of this, a thought began to form in Kilcolgan's head that something was amiss and really he should have been able to start eating by now. This little thought formed into a large enough thought that was able to stop him in his tracks and look around with what little eyesight he had.

'Who ha!' he said out loud to himself, and continued 'they Glenisheen is wanted by me for filling and then awashing down with ale. Where be their fires and houses or their place of aboding? Gone?'

Kilcolgan seriously thought that he had come to the wrong plain, and simply turned and walked back from whence he came, saying 'Who Ha!" to himself.

The Glenisheen were amazed that this had happened, as at that time Tullagh had not got around to announcing about his meeting with The

Master or the new gift. Indeed, he considered that in actual fact he may never get around to this as then he would be thought of by The Glenisheen as 'Great and Powerful Tullagh. He thus summoned the people to the City Square and mounted a platform and announced'

'I am Tullagh, your Tullagh, Tullagh the Old. I am Tullagh the Great and Powerful who will protect The Glenisheen in times of danger"

Tullagh continued. "This is the first time in the Annals of The Glenisheen that Kilcolgan has attached us and we have not suffered at all, not a Single Glenisheen was lost today and not one brick was displaced from the City of Glenisheen"

By this time the Glenisheen had thought and started to nod to each other that this was indeed the case. As they nodded they continued looking around the gathering just to check that everyone who could be there was indeed there.

"This calls for a celebration, let us all eat, drink, be merry and make music". The Glenisheen all cheered together. Only one voice of difference was raised above the crowds from Incluse, the Captain of the Guard.

"Can all the guards join in the party as well, or does Tullagh want us to continue to post lookouts on the trees, just in case Kilcolgan should hear the noise of merriment and decided to come back to investigate and have some fun of his own?"

This challenged caught Tullagh off guard and whilst he pondered how to answer he said

"Th.., th.., that's a good idea Incluse". Tullagh debated with himself if indeed he was all powerful and could hide the City again. Would the bread and bottle work again, would it work more than one time a day?, what would happen if the bottle ever ran out?, what if Kilcolgan did indeed come back and the Glenisheen found themselves too tired or drunk to offer any defence?

"I Tullagh will now answer" said Tullagh in an assertive voice. "The guards will remain posted as we Glenisheen must surely remember that whilst Kilcolgan let us unscathed today, he has still not been totally defeated. We will eat, drink and make merry and have some quiet music that will not attack Kilcolgan back to our environs"

The Glenisheen gave a muffled cheer, conscious of the fact they were back to going about their business of life in a quiet way and acknowledging the fact that they, as yet were not going to be able to have a loud party as they could not risk upsetting the neighbour.

The party did go on for several days, and over that time Tullagh was debated and discussed as being a great leader (even though he wouldn't allow the Glenisheen to have a noisy party). Tullagh meanwhile, although he joined in the party did worry that he may have made a mistake in declaring himself great and powerful in his speech and not acknowledging the real source of his power as being due to his meeting with The Master and absolutely nothing to do with himself. It was for this reason as Tullagh found himself in different houses over the days of the party he would greet the householders with the greeting 'The Master is Great and Powerful'.

It was not too long before this phrase found itself in common usage with The Glenisheen, but also not long before it was used in a banal way without thought, more or less as just something to say as one would greet someone with 'hello'. In fact some of the younger Glenisheen got fed up with what they thought was a longwinded expression, that they shortened 'The Master is Great and Powerful' to simply 'MIGAP'. Although the parents of the young Glenisheen would often chastise them for using the phrase 'Migap' as a greeting, it got to the stage before the end of the party that the parents had given up simply because it got to be the case that everyone started using the shortened version. In some cases within a few weeks, a significant number of the Glenisheen had completely forgotten what the root of the phrase was as 'Migap' became the favoured phrase of greeting.

Kilcolgan did hear the merriment at Glenisheen, but the noise confused him as he knew in his heart of hearts that the Glenisheen were a timid and fearful race that wouldn't dare to hold a party as that would indeed draw attention to themselves and lead an enemy direct to their doorstep. Therefore Kilcolgan's reasoning was that the noise was not coming from Glenisheen but from somewhere else, and for that reason Kilcolgan looked in all the opposite directions from the merriment for where Glenisheen could be. Needless to say he didn't find them but simply ended up more confused with a very sore head.

The other unhappy group were the guards, as they had to spend the entire period of the party on extra special alert as they really expected a further attack from Kilcolgan with all the (quiet) noise. The lookouts and guards were particularly annoyed as the guards that were to come to relieve them got tied up with the party and as a result the thought didn't even cross their minds to come and relieve them.

It was only when Glenisheen had settled down to get on with ordinary life and Kilcolgan got plenty of rest and let his sore head clear that he dug deep into his memories to be able to line up again at his statutory starting point and move in the actual direction of Glenisheen. In this way he was able to mount several more attacks, but needless to say that every time this happened, the lookouts were ready, the bell was rung and Tullagh could perform his ritual to make Glenisheen disappear. Although Tullagh thought that at some stage the magical potion would run out, this never happened as the bottle always appeared full whenever he took off the cork.

Tullagh was to have one further meeting with the Master one day when he was out walking with his young son, Tullagh the Young. Tullagh the Old was showing his son the beauties of the forest and the animals and birds when he came across a small brown rabbit with its front paw caught up in some brambles. Tullagh the old immediately offered assistance and was annoyed to note that he had forgotten his knife. The only thing he could think off was to break the bottle of magic potion to be able to get a sharp edge to cut through the bramble. Tullagh debated with himself as to how he could save the liquid, and he tried to do this but it soon disappeared as he worked with the sharp edge of the broken bottle to free the rabbit.

Tullagh released the poor creature and it was not long before the white tail of the rabbit was bounding back into the woods.

"Daddy, you're a hero" said the young Tullagh, clapping his hands and jumping up and down with a gleeful smile on his face.

"Now I've blown it" thought Tullagh to himself as he pondered how strange it was that his young son was so gleeful at a time when his father had just taken steps that could secure the destruction of his race. "Is the life of one rabbit more or less important than the lives of the entire Glenisheen" Tullagh continued.

Tullagh secretly hoped that this act of kindness may benefit him in some way as he never had forgotten the incident with the dwarf who later turned out to be The Master, although there was sufficient doubt in his mind as to whether or not the rabbit could have been The Master as Tullagh didn't know whether or not The Master could turn into animals such as small brown rabbits with little white tails as well as dwarf's. 'Surely a lowly rabbit would be too unimportant for The Master' Tullagh reasoned with himself. As Tullagh thought these things he noticed his young son run off after the rabbit.

'I can be whatever I want' spoke a voice to Tullagh as if it had read his thoughts. Tullagh fell to his knees as The Master had chosen that very time to appear.

'Yet again you have shown kindness and made an important sacrifice, so your heart has remained true throughout your reign as Tullagh" added the Master, and went on "for this you can choose one further gift for the Glenisheen".

Tullagh had often thought of whether or not he had made the right decision the first time he had met The Master, and asked himself why he had not simply asked for Glenisheen to be made permanently invisible to Kilcolgan during times of attack. Now faced with the offer from The Master of another gift he knew already what to ask for.

"Great Master" Tullagh said, raising his eyes to see the shining figure before him. "I thank you for your great and bountiful gifts to the Glenisheen".

"I am surprised that you are offering thanks from the Glenisheen given that only a small remnant of Glenisheen still believe in me" added The Master.

Tullagh knew that in the Annals of Glenisheen that Tullagh's traditionally meet with The Master twice during their life, once in the period immediately following the election when The Master endorses the election result and if he is pleased will bestow a gift. The second time is more worrying as the meeting takes place at a point somewhere near the end of the life of Tullagh the Old. The Annals record that at the second meeting Tullagh has to give account of how he ruled the Glenisheen. The words of The Master were worrying Tullagh.

"I am surprised at your reign Tullagh the Old". The many Tullagh's who have been elected and ruled before you have always added an account of their meetings with The Master to the Annals, and yet you chose not to do this".

"I am sorry Great Master" Tullagh said with a noticeable shudder in his voice. "I..I..."

" You do not need to tell me what you have done as I already know all!" said The Master.

"You chose to take the glory of the preservation of the Glenisheen during the first attack of your reign to yourself. The speech you gave I well remember..... I am Tullagh the Great and Powerful who will protect The Glenisheen in times of danger". It is not for you to offer protection to the Glenisheen, that is my job"

"I am really sorry oh great Master" said Tullagh.

"Do not apologise, if you were sorry you would have preserved my name and my memory. The Glenisheen have reduced my precious name to nothing, what is it?, 'MIGAP' – that sounds so ridiculous, like something one would speak of when they have lost a tooth".

Tullagh was speechless as he realised that he had failed in his reign. He kept his head down and had no words to offer.

"Despite the failings of your reign, I am aware that your heart is pure. Yes, you have made mistakes and sought to take power and glory for yourself rather than ascribing the source of your power to me. I am prepared to give you one gift to mark the end of your reign".

Tullagh knew that he would have very little time left to live following this meeting as the final gift of The Master was one which had to be written in The Annals before the Tullagh's time on earth had ended.

"Oh great Master, I truly am sorry for the failings in my life and for not ascribing the power to you. I will seek to make amends in the time that remains." Said Tullagh, as he began to feel the frailness of his body and realise that he was aging ever more rapidly than he had done up to this time.

"The one gift I respectfully request is that Glenisheen will be made permanently invisible to the eyes of Kilcolgan" asked Tullagh.

"This gift I will grant" said The Master as he suddenly disappeared.

Tullagh raised his head and saw The Master no more, but gathered his thoughts, unsure as to how Glenisheen would become invisible without the bottle of potion. Tullagh realised that his son was still missing, so he rose and began to call after him in the direction he had seed the rabbit run.

Tullagh the Young stepped out from behind a tree, holding the rabbit in his hands and stroking its large ears. This caused Tullagh some consternation as up to this point he had thought that the Rabbit was The Master in different form, but he knew that could not be the case if he had been talking to The Master and his son had been holding the rabbit.

Tullagh and his son made their way back to Glenisheen, with the father having a heavy heart and the son a skip in his small step as he was totally unaware of anything that had transpired.

On returning home Tullagh the Old immediately went to the Storeroom of the Annals and arranged for a scribe to update The Annals both in terms of his first meeting with The Master. There was a look of genuine surprise on the look of the face of the scribe as he recorded the first meeting and realised that it was not as he had been brought up to believe that it was Tullagh who was great and powerful and protected The Glenisheen, but instead The Master. The scribe also thought that it was most unfortunate that all reference to The Master in Glenisheen culture and customs had more or less disappeared and been reduced to a meaningless greeting. As the scribe listened to Tullagh record his last meeting with The Master it was with some sadness as the words recorded indicated that Tullagh would not be long for the world.

Despite these thoughts Tullagh the Old lived for a further ten human years before he would pass, and over this time his health deteriorated and he became increasingly frailer by the day. Tullagh realised his punishment from The Master as on a daily basis he begged The Master to let him die rather than let him continue in such poor health and state of frailness.

During these years Kilcolgan did try to attack, but was completely unable to locate Glenisheen, to such an extent that he would never try and attack again. Instead, he was forced to change his diet away from the protein rich Glenisheen to other means of sustenance.

Although Kilcolgan was very much a giant to the Glenisheen, one must remember that the Glenisheen were very much shorter in stature to any other race that closely resembled humankind. As for Kilcolgan, although he was a giant and a bully towards Glenisheen he also was a coward when it came to dealings with the humans. He had learned to his cost that two or three beefy humans armed with trusty pitchforks could do damage to his legs and render him unable to walk for several days. That is why Kilcolgan stayed well clear of Humans.

However, giants have to eat and eat they must. Kilcolgan needed to feed himself with at least a couple of fully grown sheep for lunch and breakfast and ideally a fully grown cow for supper. In order to survive Kilcolgan at night crept around the farms on the outside of Galway city and took much livestock and crops from the fields. The net result is that Galway became an undesirable place to live as this was the very food that was needed to ensure the survival of the city folk. Over several years the people of Galway suffered from food shortages and famine. Kilcolgan simply didn't care as his belly was full and he saw his actions of something akin to payback for the holes in his breaches and scars on his leg and buttocks from the beefy farmers and their pitchforks. 'No so beefy now, te dum' Kilcolgan would often think to himself.

* * * *

Tullagh the Old (and frail) died in his sleep one night in spring, leaving his one son who was by then aged 18 and many daughters.

* * * *

The Annals of Glenisheen stated that when a Tullagh died that he should be buried the same night and an election immediately held for a new ruler. However, in the latter years of the reign of Tullagh the Old Glenisheen had become a pitiful place as complacency, neglect and a lack of sense of direction had replaced what had been a hardworking race. Thoughts of Kilcolgan were assigned to myth and folklore as the Glenisheen let go of their sense of purpose and fighting spirit. The guards had been stood down and lookouts were no more. Even the pigeons had been allowed to fly off wild to find new homes and fend for their selves.

None of the Glenisheen ever bothered to consult The Annals to see what should have happened at that time in terms of the rites for burying a Tullagh and the rules for conducting the election, let alone when an election should be held.

For this reason it was about 6 human weeks later that Incluse, who was by then an old Glenisheen suggested that it might be a good idea to think about holding an election. Enough of the Glenisheen agreed with him on this matter and Incluse was charged with calling the election. Again, The Annals were not consulted which was another of a series of critical mistakes that would eventually herald the downfall of the Glenisheen as a race.

At election time the tradition was that a candidate would stand for election from each of the twelve families of Glenisheen, being Tullagh, Murroogh, Formoyle, Feenagh, Monien, Funshin, Mullagh, Glasgeivnagh, Noughval, Knockfin, Albadie and Funore. The Annals of Glenisheen record that it was always a Tullagh that would win the election, and always the son od the previus leader.

With The Great Peace as it had become known, belief in The Master had virtually disappeared from the minds of the Glenisheen, and along with that went any interest in reading the Annals or the tradition or custom and practice that was contained within the pages of The Annals.

The Glenisheen as a race believed that they lived in a modern society and therefore had no need to keep with the traditions of the past, such as electing another Tullagh. There was much talk about a 'time for change' and 'looking to the future' along with the need for 'dynamic new leadership' and one of the candidates – Knockfin even talked in terms of 'a new Glenisheen Order'.

The debates around the time of the election were fuelled by the fact that the logical successor to Tullagh the Old was not a popular candidate, as he was generally regarded as being lazy, arrogant and proud. Although most of the people had more or less forgotten the old threat from Kilcolgan, some of the older Glenisheen did debate as the sun went down the fact that 'this Tullagh has never proved himself in battle', although battle against what was unknown.

As the time of Election Day grew nearer a new wind blew through the city of Glenisheen whereby candidates from each of the twelve families started making speeches on the street corners and putting up posters of themselves around the walls of the City. This was new as in the past it had more or less been taken for granted that the Tullagh would automatically be elected and therefore none of the other token candidates bothered to do much about the election. This year was different. As time went on it began to be apparent that the most popular candidate was not going to be Tullagh but most likely the Knockfin candidate. The reasons for this were varied, with some Glenisheen favouring his powers of oratory (and the idea of a new order), others (mainly girls) commenting on his locks of long brown curly hair and fair complexion or some just mentioning that Knockfin was a good hunter and therefore 'would be best able to provide for the Glenisheen in times of scarcity'.

The talk of 'better times under Knockfin' was quite strange as under the rule of Tullagh's the Glenisheen had always been well provided for and had never suffered scarcity. The idea of scarcity was one which could only have come from the world of men given the fact that Glenisheen were becoming braver and would often travel further afield than the environs of Glenisheen, and some had even found human settlement where there was indeed much talk of 'scarcity' which fell on the ears of these brave Glenisheen as they listened at the doors in secret.

Knockfin's position was the candidate of choice was further strengthened by events that occurred two days before Election Day. Knockfin was walking in the woods one misty morning, and as he rested to smoke his pipe and listen to the birdsong, he was surprised to note that two crows sitting on a tree branch in front of his eyes were speaking in a language that he could understand. Knockfin stood very still so as to not scare away the birds and he listened intently.

"Did you hear that the Tullagh of Glenisheen has passed?" asked the first bird.

"Aye, that I did" responded the second bird.

"What will that mean for the Glenisheen I wonder?" asked the first bird.

"Frightening times ahead I'm sure" said the second bird.

"What do you mean?" asked the first

"Sure don't you know that once the Tullagh dies that any of the gifts given from The Master disappear until the new Tullagh has proven himself?" said the second.

"Are you serious?" asked the first as the second bird cocked his head up and down as if to answer yes,

"What will that mean for the Glenisheen then?" asked the second.

"No more invisible Glenisheen the, and Kilcolgan will come storming over the plain and it will be Glenisheen for breakfast, lunch and supper again" said the first bird.

"When will this happen then?" asked the second bird.

"I have heard it in the wind that The Master has deafened and blinded Kilcolgan for four days, and then he will attack" said the first bird.

Knockfin had heard enough of what he considered to be bad luck tittle tattle from the birds, and so to end the conversation he took out his crossbow and loaded a double headed arrow and shot the both birds firmly through their breasts.

Knockfin was still worried by the conversation, and so he ran back to Glenisheen as fast as his legs would carry him and ran to the square and began to ring the warning bell. No sound came from the bell, and Knockfin saw a sign on the wall beside the rope

'We the people of Glenisheen have such faith in our Great Tuillagh, that this warning bell that once told of the forthcoming attack of a Giant called Kilcolgan is no longer needed. For this reason we have removed the hammer from the bell'

Knockfin was amazed, and he had to run to the local blacksmith's shop where he lifted a heavy hammer and then ran to the top of the bell tower and started striking the bell to attract attention.

Although most of the Glenisheen by this stage had never heard the bell ring, they responded anyway thinking that something important was going to happen, and as they arrived in the square, Knockfin could be seen standing at the top of the bell tower.

Knockfin's face was bright red, beads of sweat were dripping from his brow and he spoke in short sharp bursts.

"Glenisheen I must address you" he said.

"Speak up" said a voice from the crown. Knockfin caught his breath and began to speak with more authority.

"Glenisheen" he continued. "I am the bearer of news. I have found on the wind (he didn't want to say that he had killed the crows) that the giant Kilcolgan is real and is not simply a tale that we scare our children with. This giant knows of the death of Tullagh and will come to attack our beloved city in four days from hence."

By this stage a number of voices in the assembly could be heard saying meaningful words such as 'oh' and 'uum' as they realised that this was not going to be an election speech about the new order of Glenisheen.

"We must examine The Annals" said Knockfin, "we might just find that the last Tullagh met The Master and was given a gift from The Master of making Glenisheen invisible during times of attack. Glenisheen can now be seen by all and sundry including Kilcolgan the giant who is coming to attack"

"What shall we do?" asked the Glenisheen?

"Let's hold the election today, so that we can have a leader that can manage this situation" offered

Knockfin, when in reality he knew that he had no answers.

"We don't need an election, we need ideas for action" shouted a voice from the crowd.

"Let us raise a guard....., and post lookouts ..... and defend ourselves" said Knockfin nervously.

"We have no guard, we have no lookouts, we have no weapons" said the Glenisheen in response. Knockfin knew that he had no answers and was spend, so he simply fell to the ground and nursed his knees in his arms with his head bowed.

It was at that precise moment that Tullagh the young decided to stop being lazy and proud and arrogant, and walked up to steps of the bell tower and stood behind the sunken Knockfin.

"I am Tullagh of the Tullagh, the proud family that has ruled Glenisheen since Glenisheen were born as a race" said Tullagh.

"Whilst all of you were listening to the empty rhetoric of the speeches from candidates at this election, I have not been making speeches". Said Tullagh.

"Whilst you were debating empty promises of what the future would look like I have been reading The Annals" Tullagh went on "I may have appeared proud as I knew what the questions were and what the answers are as well, for these truths are contained in the pages of The Annals."

By this time some in the crowd were showing disinterest, others had turned their backs to walk away, and others were more concerned with a possible attack of an old enemy that the myths and legends that Tullagh was now speaking.

"Don't walk away from your Tullagh" said Tullagh with considerable authority as his confidence grew due to his realisation of the seriousness of what Knockfin had communicated.

"For many years I have maintained my silence. I have never spoken of these things until now, but now is the time to reveal great secrets" said Tullagh, and by this time he had the attention of the assembly.

"Many years ago when I was a young child, my father Tullagh the Old made a great sacrifice in the forest, where he saved a poor creature from ensnarement". This was simply a little rabbit which ran off through the forest without a care in the world apart from a sore paw" Tullagh continued.

"Being a young child I ran after the rabbit to see where it would go, but I soon lost it, and so I returned to the place where I had left my father. There I saw a sight that I have never spoken off due to feat. My father Tullagh the Old was taking with The Master, yes, The Master – he is real!"

"Even my Father did not know that I saw the events of that day or heard the conversations about the City of Glenisheen being invisible to all" said Tullagh,

"When they had finished talking The Master simply disappeared, but I looked at my feet and there was the rabbit that I had been chasing. I picked it up and as I did so a voice came from the rabbit which was the same voice that The Master had used. I was told not to say anything about the events until such times as this bell rang again. Today is the day"

The crowd by this stage were flabbergasted, with some carrying expressions of bewilderment and wonder whilst others were standing with their eyes wide open staring at Tullagh.

"Tullagh for Tullagh" cried one voice from the crown.

"No!" answered another "He's lazy"

"He can't hunt" shouted another voice whilst at the same time another vice called 'Tullagh for Tullagh"

No, No, No!" cried another voice "He is much too proud to be Tullagh – just listen to his pride now" he added whilst another cry went up of 'Tullagh for Tullagh".

Even with the voices of dissention in the crowd, it was not too long before the cries of "Tullagh for Tullagh" were chanting in unison and the dissenting voices were drowned out.

Knockfin rose to his feet and lifted the right arm of Tullagh into the Air. "Tullagh for Tullagh" he cried at the top of his voice as the crowd looked on in amazement. Knockfin was glad to be able to divert the crowd's attention from himself as he really had run out of ideas.

The crown acknowledged Knockfin's stance as saying that he didn't want to be part of the election anymore and this was an endorsement of Tullagh to be the new leader.

"Who votes for Tullagh to be Tullagh" shouted Knockfin over the crowd, and a resounding "Aye" was heard from the majority of those present.

"I proclaim Tullagh to be leader" shouted Knockfin and the crowd cheered.

Meanwhile, The Master had been watching the evens in the city square with interest, and at that moment in time decided to intervene and appear to Tullagh.

Although Tullagh could see him, the entire crowd simply froze in time with whatever they were doing.

"Very good rousing" said the Master to Tullagh "and a very good attempt to turn many years of neglect f the Glenisheen towards the direction that theur loyalty should be at" he continued.

"Thank You Master, one does one's best" said Tullagh.

"Yes indeed Tullagh, I have noticed that you are a proud Glenisheen and have not learned that pride can lead to a fall, you would be well advised to remember that" said The Master.

"Allk right then I will Master" said Tullagh impatiently.

"Is this when you offer me a gift and I ask that Kilcolgan be defeated, and you say that the gift of defeating Kilcolgan is not within your power and I then think of another one?" continued Tullagh, hardly waiting to catch his breath.

"You have been reading The Annals Tullagh, but whilst you know of history you are also very impatient, but to save time I will offer you a gift!" said The Master.

"Right then, quite simply the gift I ask is that you would make me twice as tall in stature as what Kilcolgan is" asked Tullagh.

"So be it" said the Master who quickly disappeared and at the same time Tullagh began to grow- slowly at first and then suddenly, only to find that his clothes were ripped to shreds in the process and feel from his body. He stood then naked the same height as some of the tress of the forest.

Tullagh turned and began striding back to the City of Glenisheen, proud of his new stature. As some of the Glenisheen saw him coming they were terrified thinking that this was indeed Kilcolgan who was striding towards them. Tullagh was shocked to see the expressions on their faces and then took account of the fact he was naked and the Glenisheen didn't recognise him.

"Fear not!" said Tullagh, "It is I, your Tullagh – only taller than what you remember", his voice booming out across the city.

Many of the worried Glenisheen recognised his voice and felt a little more at ease. Although Tullagh was now too tall to enter the City, he lay down outside the wall to preserve his modesty and also to be able to address the Glenisheen at something near eye level.

"I have met The Master and received his gift" said Tullagh as the Glenisheen listened intently.

"Pith you didn't receive a new cloak to go with it" said one of the Glenisheen women who stood on the city wall, nodding in the direction of Tullagh's nakedness.

"There is nothing I can do about that" said Tullagh realising his embarrassing predicament.

The Glenisheen woman called down to the crowd at the foot of the wall. "Assemble the women of the twelve families with nimble fingers for sewing, and get them all to bring whatever spare cloaks they have in their abodes. We need to make a super cloak for Tullagh", and with that she went down the steps from the wall to run to her own home to gather her materials. Many women then began cutting and sewing to make the largest Glenisheen cloak they had ever seen. Before nightfall this was ready for Tullagh.

During this time Tullagh continued to talk to the assembled Glenisheen. Plans were discussed as to what to do in preparation for the imminent attack of Kilcolgan. It was decided that there was no time left to fashion weapons and that the best defence would be the sheer size of Tullagh. As night fell and Tullagh donned his new cloak, which made him look something like a Friesian cow from the world of humans due to the mixture of black and white summer and winter cloaks. Other that the strange design it fitted him perfectly. However, it was then that Tullagh began to realise his mistake – as he was too large to enter the City of Glenisheen let alone sleep on a Glenisheen sized bed, he was faced with no option but to lie outside the city walls and sleep on the ground.

Tullagh's tallness became the point of discussion in many a home after dark as the Glenisheen retired for the night. 'How will we feed him?' asked one, and another answered 'he may go and steal from the Humans as one meal for him may be a year's supply for the entire city" added another. 'Where's he going to live? He will need a very tall house and all of his furniture enlarged as well" commented a wise old Glenisheen, but it was one of the women who came up with another problem., whilst a group of her friends were discussing the parts of his body that were no larger than normal. "Hey!" the woman said rasing her voice, and continued when she had achieved silence "Tullagh is not married and has no son to succeed him in the next election – just how is this going to happen now?" The laughter than had being taking place up to that point was suddenly subdued as the implications of this statement began to enter the psyche of the Glenisheen women.

"But there has always been a Tullagh heir to succeed his father, what happens then?" Although the debate went on that actual realisation of the implication was not identified.

Four days passed, by which time there was much debate and Tullagh ate well, although by this time it was taking an army of Glenisheen to keep him provided for. By the time the four days we up, Tullagh was up early in the morning before sunrise, standing in the plain with lookouts posted in the tress around the end of the forest. Quite why he did this remains a mystery as Tullagh had a view well over the tops of most of the tress.

In a cave at the foot of the Lough Corrib, Kilcolgan regained his sight and hearing and soon picked up from the whispers in the trees that Tullagh was dead and that the Glenisheen had ceased to become invisible. Before too long Kilcolgan had lit a torch from his fire and gathered a giant spear and was charging across the forest and plan intent on destroying the Glenisheen finally.

Tullagh saw Kilcolgan as he made his charge, and shouted across the trees to him, "Kilcolgan, come and meet your doom".

At first Kilcolgan didn't even hear Tullagh let alone pay him any attention, given the fact that even though his hearing and eyesight had returned, they were not up to scratch and the poor light of the morning made objects appear as shadows.

"Kil...Col...Gan.." booked Tullagh, and this time Kilcolgan heard him and slowed slightly to place his head in each direction of the compass to see who was calling him.

"Kil..Col,..Gan.. Come and meet your end" shouted Tullagh again. It was easy for Tullagh to see where Kilcolgan was coming from given the torch of fire in his hand.

Before long the full fury of the battle was unleased. Although Tullagh was much taller than Kilcolgan he didn't use his height to his full advantage. It was as if he hadn't come to terms with his new size and the size itself was proving to be a hindrance as Tullagh clumsily threw himself around, at first to attack Kilcolgan and then to defend himself.

Kilcolgan was battled hardened and the bulges in his arms and leg were pure muscle that hadn't softened any in the years he had not done battle with the Glenisheen. He wounded Tullagh with hard high punches to the stomach and even managed to jump high enough to grab a handful of Tullagh's hair and pull his face nearer the ground to land more punches on his cheekbones and around his eyes. Blood started to gush from Tullagh's face, as he reeled backwards thinking to himself that his plan to defeat Kilcolgan was well and truly backfiring. Tullagh considered the difference between him and the battle hardened giant. 'Perhaps the Glenisheen had a point in not wanting to elect me as I hadn't been in battle' he thought to himself, just in time to see Kilcolgan come running at him again, with his torch in hand.

'Burn you monster' shouted Kilcolgan as the torch was shoved in the direction of Tullagh's face, but

Tullagh had seen this coming and managed to grab the torch and wrench it from Kilcolgan's hand.

'Not today little giant' said Tullagh in between puffs of breath. The torch meanwhile had sailed out of his hand and landed in the City of Glenisheen where it set fire to buildings in its wake.

Kilcolgan retreated a short distance from this encounter and bent to lif a large boulder that was in the plain, which he lifted above his head and lunged at Tullagh. Unfortunately Tullagh had his back to Kilcolgan at the time, watching the devastation that was starting to unfold beneath his feet in Glenisheen. The boulder smashed the back of Tullagh's head and knocked him to the ground, Tullagh felt the sharp pain at the back of his head as his body fell to the ground, destroying part of the city wall and the houses he landed on.

'Size doesn't matter when you've never fought Kilcolgan' taunted the giant from the plain, convinced that he had killed Tullagh.

'You know what men say?' continued Kilcolgan, 'biggest they come hardest they fall, and just look at you, doing my job for me, how may Glenisheen have you killed today by burning their houses and falling on them?' Even though Kilcolgan thought that Tullagh was dead, he hadn't quite realised that if Tullagh was dead indeed that he would not be able to hear any of this.

Tullagh gave a stir and could just make out the end of Kilcolgan's taunts as his thoughts returned to the task at hand.

Kilcolgan saw the stirring and realised that Tullagh was not dead. 'Aw just look at you stirring like a baby getting out of its crib' continued Kilcolgan whilst realising that the battle was going to continue.

Kilcolgan was losing power as well, as hurtling the boulder had taken more out of him that he realised. He didn't want to get up close to Tullagh again in case he ran out of strength at the wrong moment, so he reasoned that another weapon was needed. There were no more boulders visible, just the grass on the plain. 'Um, grass no good' said Kilcolgan to himself as he turned and began to bound towards the tree line. 'Tree spar will have to do' he said as on reaching the tree line he bent low and began pulling at the root of a tall tree. It was not long before the tree came up by the roots. Kilcolgan had wanted to break the tree and really didn't want the roots, but his failing strength prevented this. Kilcolgan began tearing at the branches of the tree to make a better weapon than a tree, and while his mind was on this he didn't see Tullagh make his way to his feet and come across the plain with something under his arm. The noise of burning and crumbling buildings from Glenisheen masked the sound of Tullagh's heavy footsteps.

Kilcolgan noticed a shadow pass in front of him as Tullagh blocked out the light from the sun, and he turned, clumsily swinging the tree, minus its branches but complete with its roots in the direction of Tullagh's legs as clods of soil and rock fell to the ground. The effect was minimal and the tree only slightly bruised Tullagh's leg, causing him a little pain but no real damage.

What Kilcolgan didn't get time to see was that as he was so obsessed with his tree that the boulder that he had lunged at Tullagh was taken from under Tullagh's arm, at the same moment that Kilcolgan was swinging the tree around for another blow, Tullagh lifted the boulder above his head with two hands and brought it crashing down on Kilcolgan's skull before the tree had another chance to make contact with his leg.

The tree dropping from Kilcolgan's hands was the first sign that something significant had happened. The next sign was that his arms fell to his sine and then Kilcolgan dropped heavily to his needs and bowed his head as blood started leaking from his cracked skull. The next thing was that his body followed the course of his knees as he fell headlong to the ground with his arms by his side and as his face hit the ground it gouged out a trench of soil as broken teeth fell from his mouth with yet more blood.

Tullagh wasn't going to assume that Kilcolgan had given up, despite the cracked skull and now broken jaw. He wanted to make absolutely sure that Kilcolgan was finally dead, so summoning the remaining strength he had he bent low and lifted Kilcolgan's broken body, first to his chest and then with a quick change of position hoisted it above his head. Tullagh dug deep to his reserves of strength and let out an almighty cry as he launched Kilcolgan's body through the air in the direction of the tree line of the forest.

The spear that Kilcolgan had wanted to fashion from the tall tress had not been able to save him, and now those same trees would be the instruments of his final defeat. What little life was left in him it any at all was extinguished as his body fell on top of the trees which then speared him. Kilcolgan's body was left half way between the ground and the top of the tress as the lower branches acted as a buffer to stop him hitting the ground.

Tullagh did not fully believe that this marked the end, and he continued to stand rooted to the spot and stare in silence at Kilcolgan's body, half expecting it to rise and start battle again. But no movement came. Kilcolgan, who had fought countless generations of Glenisheen was finally dead at an age of several thousand years.

Still Tullagh did not move. Exhausted by the struggle. Blood continued to pour from his head. Every bone in his body ached. He was immune to the cries of the Glenisheen as their beloved city continued to burn to the ground. Only slowly, very slowly did the cries of the Glenisheen reach his ears, and he turned to look at the city, not fully taking account of the devastation before him.

Tullagh walked back over the plain towards the city with every step hurting from where Kilcolgan's tree had hit his leg, his eyes surveyed the city, fires were burning everywhere, Glenisheen were running in all directions, terrified and not knowing where to go. No one in the city had seen the defeat of Kilcolgan due to their preoccupation with their own safety. Parts of the wall lay in ruins. A number of thought's ran through Tullagh's head, 'I must save Glenisheen', but then it came to him that he couldn't enter the city due to his size. 'water' he thought, but the only source of water in the city was the well, and as he cast his eyes to where it should have been, all he saw was a pile of rubble where his fall had not only crushed the buildings but the well itself. The precious bell tower was also lying in a pile of rubble with the bell nothing more that a crushed piece of metal that would never ring again. The two things which were most precious to the Glenisheen were no more, the items which had sustained them were gone. Tullagh had no thought as to how he could fix this critical situation. There was no other water supply for miles he reasoned, apart from the water in the sea at Galway Bay, and even with this he had no means by which to transport the water overland to pour on the fires. His thoughts were confused, 'no point in bringing salt water anyway, it is fresh water that is needed for survival'. Clearly the blow to his head was affecting his reasoning.

Tullagh continued to walk across the plain and came to the walls of Glenisheen, where he paused and then began walking round. 'Do something!' came a cry, 'save us' came another, but Tullagh had no clue as to what to do. He thought back to his reading of the Annals of Glenisheen, was there anything there to give him guidance, no, only how to defend the city from the attack of Kilcolgan but nothing, no nothing about how to save a city that was burning.

The fire was causing such mayhem that hot ashes and embers were rising into the air and falling on the plain and into the trees of the forest where they soon set more fires and large areas were soon ablaze. Even if Tullagh could have made his way to a water source, the route was soon blocked by an inferno in the forest, it was this inferno that consumed the broken body of Kilcolgan as it caught fire and exploded in a green haze.

Tullagh continued pacing around the city walls, occasionally having to swipe burning embers from his cloak and hair. His senses became numb and it was not too long before he felt no pain as his body's nervous system was in overload.

His thoughts faded and turned to The Master.

'Master, where are you?' he said in a whisper that could be barely heard above the noise. 'Master, where are you?' he said a few more times, but no one could hear him apart from himself, and at times he wasn't sure whether he was hearing his voice or imagining that he was hearing the conversation with himself in his head.

Confusion reigned. 'It wasn't the Master that defeated Kilcolgan, it was me!, and now the Glenisheen can live in peace' Tullagh thought as he continued his pacing. His pace had slowed down and continued to slow.

'Pride?, Ha!, who needed The Master' he said between sharp gasps of breath. 'Meant to be there to….. to protect…Glenisheen….where was he…...'

As is a question was asked by an invisible being Tullagh heard a voice in his head saying 'are you proud'

'Proud…?' asked Tullagh in response, 'who…wants…to..know' he gasped, but no one answered.

'How can …I be proud?' Tullagh asked himself, 'I … am…too…too… big … to be any ….use' he said as he slowed down further. 'I…have destroyed…Glenisheen, not…Kilcolgan' his discourse continued.

'You must be proud' said the voice in his head.

'You are the one, the only Tullagh to defeat Kilcolgan' the voice continued.

'Yes..' said Tullagh as he stopped with his legs sinking under him. His face was now covered in blood from the gash in his head.

'I didn't need…. Master….in the end…I was the one … that ended….Kil..col..gan'

Tullagh summoned what little strength he had left in his body and cried

'Yes, I AM PROUD'.

These were the last words he uttered as his body crashed to the ground, landing face down on top of what was left of Glenisheen. Fire licked around his body, but Tullagh did not feel it as he was gone, he had no son, the last of the Tullaghs.

Glenisheen was silent. Most Glenisheen were now dead, and those that were not were too stupefied to speak as they felt the shake of Tullagh's body reverberate through the foundations of the city.

The initial crash subsided to be replaced by a low rumbling sound from deep inside the earth. The rumbling was barely audible at first but it grew in intensity and as it did so the ground began to shake, not perceivably at first but then the entire ground began to shake as the surface of the land began to buckle and rumble. What was left on any building or wall in Glenisheen came crashing to the ground killing whoever was left of the Glenisheen. Then, with a mighty roar the entire surface of the plain and the city began to move. While the north side raised high into the air, the south began to sink deep into the earth. It was as if a hinge had been fixed at some point far underneath Glenisheen that the entire plain was now pivoting on. The north continued its rise, and at one point the body of Tullagh slipped from the surface of the land along with the rubble that had been Glenisheen and the bodies of many thousands and fell into the abyss that the movement the land had created.

The displaced land sat upright when it reached its peak, totally upright whilst the last of what had been Glenisheen, the plain and the forest slipped from the surface deep underground. The burning trees followed the debris deep underground where the fires merged into a monster fire that consumed all that fed it. The flames could be seen rising to the top of the higher most part of the land that was pointing upwards as every blade of grass was consumed.

After what seemed like an eternity, the flames from the fire retired underground and several different colours of smoke emerged. Although the day had been clear and sunny to begin with, the sky could not be seen due to the pallor of smoke.

The fractured land did not move and slowly a gentle hint of a breeze began to blow, moving the smoke in the direction of the sea. It was this breeze that collided with the upright land and started it moving again. At first, almost unnoticed what had been the surface of the land began a slow descent towards the abyss, and what had been up to this point the underground part of the structure began to move upwards. The structure only slowly increased in speed and is it approached the horizontal it slowed again like a door closing.

The surface of the land was transformed. The rocks that had been deep underground and forming the bedrock of the land were now exposed to the surface, grey and wrinkled like the face of a Glenisheen. There was not a piece of vegetation seen anywhere, just endless miles of grey wrinkled rocks, a landscape that resembled the surface of the moon, devoid of life, dry, barren. That is the way The Burren looks today and there are only a few places where any vegetation has been able to take hold.

****

Those of us who listened to the story in McDermott's that night had not noticed the hours slipping away. The sun had set, darkness had come, and now the morning was approaching as the first hints of sunrise began to appear. The story had gone on all night and we had sat transfixed. No one had thought to remind us to place our last orders, or remove ourselves from McDermotts to allow the landlord to close. Time had taken on an entity of nothing as it was not recorded that night.

Ben paused as if to let the significance of the tale sink in, before adding.

"The Burren…., that name came from the time of the Glenisheen, and it simply means The Burning, except as time has went on the locals made it shorter to just The Burren. That was the end of the

Glenisheen. As a race they were extinct, wiped from the face of the earth, due to not following The Master, relying on their own strength and the last Tullagh being too proud".

"This is all well and good" said Gabriel, 'another daft Irish story of little people, just to amuse the visitors'. He paused with a half-smile on his face. "I'm surprised that you haven't published the story, set up a visitor's centre and started selling Glenisheen dolls, teddies and t-shirts" he added with a laugh.

To the rest of us, we didn't join in the laughter, almost fearing some payback from the landscape of Galway Bay for daring to poke fun at the Glenisheen. The joke rested with Gabriel as he faced blank stares from the rest of us.

"You will not find the story written anywhere' said Ben in a calm voice, and continued 'the lessons of the mistakes of the past are best remembered and not reduced to recording in a book, some people will not take the time to read the lessons, and for this reason it is better that the story be told".

The group considered Ben's philosophy.

"Aye, I suppose" said Gabriel, feeling that it was easier to accept the statement in order that the eyes of those staring at him would be redirected.

'Thank you for the story Ben" I said, trying to redeem the situation.

"Do well to remember it" Ben said.

"I will" I replied.

"Yo!, Ben" said Eamon, '"Can you tell me something, how come you know of the Glenisheen, surely there were no witnesses and they were all destroyed?"

"Indeed they were" replied Ben

"Well?" asked Eamon, not wanting to give up on this.

"There are mysteries beyond the knowledge of humans, and this is a mystery that I will choose not to relate" added Ben with a half-smile on his face.

Eamon realised that he was getting nowhere with this.

"Just leave it" I said to Eamon.

"A wise thing to do" said Ben, before adding "It is about time I moved on, the sun is nearly up". He got up and retrieved his jacket from the back of his chair which he put on. He then lifted his pipe from the table and tapped out the spend tobacco in the astray before placing the pipe in the pocket of his jacket.

"Thank you for the story" I said

"Pleasure" said Ben as he held out his right hand for me to shake.

"Ben Masterson" he said with a smile on his face, as some of the first rays of the rising son came through the window and illuminated his face in a golden yellow hue that made it seem as if some heavenly body had caused his face to shine upon this storyteller in a way that was confirming his story as true and offering a blessing on the fact that a mystery so long buried had finally been revealed. In the light of the morning face of Ben Masterson no longer looked old as it had done in the evening light, but rather youthful and mischievous as if it had been in some way been reborn. Those of us who had voluntarily given up a night's sleep to learn of one of the deep secrets of Galway Bay felt the waves of tiredness roll over us as Ben Masterson turned his face from us and walked out the back door as we were blinded by the rays of the sun streaming through the door and window.